Miss Malarkey's
FIELD TRIP

Miss Malarkey's
FIELD TRIP

Judy Finchler and
Kevin O'Malley

Illustrations by Kevin O'Malley

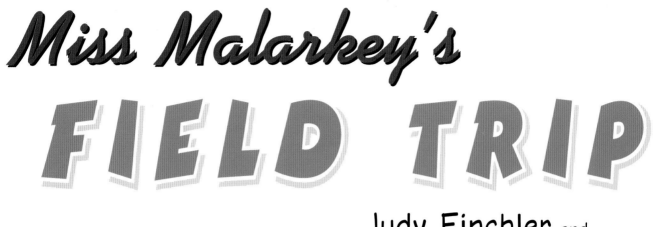

Walker & Company
New York

To my first love, Jerry, and my newest one, granddaughter Shari Nicole—you both are a source of joy! —J. F.

To Melissa T. —K. O.

First published in the United States of America in 2004 by
Walker Publishing Company, Inc.

Published simultaneously in Canada by Fitzhenry and Whiteside, Markham, Ontario L3R 4T8

For information about permission to reproduce selections from
this book, write to Permissions, Walker & Company, 104 Fifth Avenue, New York, New York 10011

Library of Congress Cataloging-in-Publication Data

Finchler, Judy.
Miss Malarkey's field trip / written by Judy Finchler and Kevin O'Malley ; illustrations by Kevin O'Malley.
p. cm.
Summary: Miss Malarkey takes her class on a field trip to the science museum, where they explore a dinosaur exhibit, watch a 3-D movie, and have many other adventures, both planned and unplanned.
ISBN 0-8027-8912-9 (HC) — ISBN 0-8027-8913-7 (RE)
[1. Field trips—Fiction. 2. Museums—Fiction. 3. Teachers—Fiction. 4. Schools—Fiction. 5. Humorous stories.] I. O'Malley, Kevin, 1961– II. Title.

PZ7.F495666M1 2004
[Fic]—dc22
2003064521

The artist used watercolors and colored pencil to create the illustrations for this book.

Book design by Nicole Gastonguay

Visit Walker & Company's Web site at www.walkeryoungreaders.com

Printed in Hong Kong

2 4 6 8 10 9 7 5 3 1

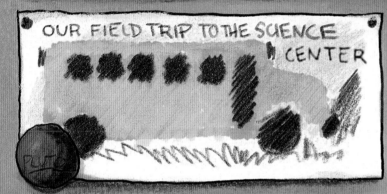

This year our class gets to go on a field trip to the science center.

Einstein

So we've been studying a lot of science.

Everybody made name tags. Then Miss Malarkey assigned each of us a buddy.

Kevin and Pat were partners.

Daniel was with Shari.

I was with Lindsay.

Every group got a chaperone.

We were all pretty excited, and it got kind of loud.

When we got off the bus everybody had to go to the bathroom. Miss Malarkey said we looked like we were dancing.

The science center has a lot of stuff that shows how our bodies work.
Miss Malarkey started to explain where earwax comes from, but she had
to stop when Jake got his arm stuck in a giant ear.

We went to the dinosaur room. I really like dinosaurs. They're very cool and scary.

Miss Malarkey started to say, "Dinosaurs lived a long time ago—"

But she had to stop when Allie decided to bury Zachary, then dig him up.

The electricity room had this awesome machine. When you touched it your hair stood up. I thought it would hurt, but it didn't even tickle.

When Miss Malarkey touched the machine . . .

The museum had a sports room, where you could
see how strong you are.

In the astronomy room, Hayley tried on a space suit. It was way too big.

Is anybody
out there?

Sarah and Brianna disappeared, but Miss Malarkey found them in the gift shop.

One of our chaperones, Mr. Spinefree, got lost in the rain forest room.
I don't think he likes lizards very much.

Miss Malarkey got sort of mad at another chaperone, Mrs. Hanoyin, because she kept talking and talking and talking.

We ate lunch in a big cafeteria. It was very noisy. Big kids from another school were throwing food and falling out of their chairs and making animal noises. They were pretty funny. Miss Malarkey didn't eat much, and it sort of looked like she was holding her head so it wouldn't fall off.

After lunch we saw a 3-D movie on a giant screen. Miss Malarkey warned us, "Sometimes movies like this can upset your stomach. Let me know if you need me to take you outside."

The movie was great. It was about flying. Miss Malarkey didn't like it so much. Her face looked a little weird, and she was holding on to her head again.

On the way back from the science center Miss Malarkey asked us what we had learned on our field trip.

We had a great time on our field trip. And the day got even better when Miss Malarkey told us we wouldn't have any homework.

After school was over I peeked in the classroom window to see if Miss Malarkey was OK. She was holding her head but . . .

she was smiling.